Freya the Brave

by Damian Harvey and Max Rambaldi

FRANKLIN WATTS
LONDON • SYDNEY

Many years ago, there lived a Viking girl

named Freya. Her father was Olaf the Strong.

He was a brave warrior, and chief of the village.

Her mother had been a brave warrior too,

but she had died when Freya was a baby.

Freya's older brothers, Erik and Ivan,

were always arguing about

which of them was the bravest.

Freya tried hard to be brave,

but inside she felt small and scared.

One evening, Chief Olaf called all the Vikings to the great hall.

"My sons and I are going on a voyage to seek new land," he said. "Who will join us?"

Many of the Vikings raised their hands, showing they wanted to go.
So did Freya.

"You can't come," said Erik.

"You're a girl," grinned Ivan.

"That's not fair," cried Freya.

"I can be brave, too."

"You are brave," said Chief Olaf.

"Just like your mother. But I want you
to stay here where it's safe."

The next day, the ship was loaded,

ready for the trip.

There were barrels of smoked fish,

and fresh water for the voyage.

There were tools to build a camp.

There were hens and goats so the warriors

would have eggs and milk on their journey.

When they were ready to set sail,

Chief Olaf looked around for Freya,

so he could say goodbye, but he could not see

his daughter anywhere. He did not think

of looking under the pile of furs.

Freya had hidden herself

there and fallen asleep.

Freya woke to the sound of crashing thunder.

Lightning lit the sky and the wind howled.

As she watched the storm, a huge wave

washed over the ship's deck.

Then she heard a cry.

A wave had carried Chief Olaf into the sea.

Freya leapt to her feet.

"Quick!" she cried.

"We must save him."

But the other Vikings

did not know

what to do.

As quick as she could, Freya picked up a rope

and threw one end to her father. As soon as

he grabbed it, she pulled him back in.

Two of the warriors helped her.

Her brothers stood and watched as

Chief Olaf was hauled back on to the ship.

"Thank you, Freya," gasped Olaf.

Suddenly, high above their heads, there was

a loud crack. Everyone looked up.

The strong wind had broken the top of the mast.

"Someone will have to fix it," cried Freya.

"I can't climb," said Erik, with a worried look.

"I don't like heights," said Ivan.

"What about you, Rolf?" said Freya
to the tallest Viking. "You're tall and strong."

Everyone watched as Rolf climbed the mast.

The wind blew and the waves crashed,

but he still managed to fix it.

The Vikings cheered.

"I could have done that," said Erik.

The next day, one of the Vikings spotted

something in the sea.

"Sea monster!" he yelled.

"It will eat the ship," said Ivan.

"It will eat us!" cried Erik.

The Vikings did not know what to do

and hid behind their shields.

Then Freya had an idea.

She took the lid off a big barrel

and plunged her hand inside.

"Help me throw some fish," she cried.

Freya pulled out a handful of dried fish
and threw it as far out to sea as she could.
The other Vikings did the same.

The huge sea monster swam after the fish

and the Vikings all cheered.

Freya had saved them again.

"I could have done that," said Ivan.

Chief Olaf sat Freya on his shoulder.

"You're the bravest of us all," he said.

"No, I'm not," Freya smiled.

"But together we can all be brave."

Then Freya spotted something.

"Land," she cried.

The Vikings cheered again.

"This is just the start of our adventure,"

said Chief Olaf.

Story order

Look at these 5 pictures and captions.
Put the pictures in the right order
to retell the story.

1

Freya saved her father from the sea.

2

Freya sent Rolf to fix the mast.

3

Freya hid on the ship.

4

Freya threw fish to the sea monster.

5

Freya was not allowed to go on the voyage.

Independent Reading

This series is designed to provide an opportunity for your child to read on their own. These notes are written for you to help your child choose a book and to read it independently.

In school, your child's teacher will often be using reading books which have been banded to support the process of learning to read. Use the book band colour your child is reading in school to help you make a good choice. *Freya the Brave* is a good choice for children reading at Gold Band in their classroom to read independently.

The aim of independent reading is to read this book with ease, so that your child enjoys the story and relates it to their own experiences.

About the book

Freya longs to go on the voyage with her father and brothers, but she is not allowed. So she hides away on the ship and soon proves just how brave she can be.

Before reading

Help your child to learn how to make good choices by asking: "Why did you choose this book? Why do you think you will enjoy it?" Look at the cover together and ask: "What do you think the story will be about?" Ask your child to think of what they already know about the Vikings. Then ask your child to read the title aloud. Ask: "Do you think Freya looks brave on the cover?" Remind your child that they can sound out the letters to make a word if they get stuck.

Decide together whether your child will read the story independently or read it aloud to you.

During reading

Remind your child of what they know and what they can do independently. If reading aloud, support your child if they hesitate or ask for help by telling the word. If reading to themselves, remind your child that they can come and ask for your help if stuck.

After reading

Support comprehension by asking your child to tell you about the story. Use the story order puzzle to encourage your child to retell the story in the right sequence, in their own words. The correct sequence can be found on the next page.

Help your child think about the messages in the book that go beyond the story and ask: "Why do you think Freya's brothers are always saying that they could have done the things she did? Do you think she is braver than her older brothers?"

Give your child a chance to respond to the story: "What do you think being brave means? At the start of the story, Freya does not seem brave, but she does some very brave things. Have you ever had to be brave about doing something? How do you help yourself feel brave?"

Extending learning

Help your child predict other possible outcomes of the story by asking: "If Freya had not been brave, what do you think might have happened? Do you think the other Vikings would have been braver? Would they have had to act quicker if Freya had not saved them each time?"

In the classroom, your child's teacher may be teaching contractions. There are many examples in this book that you could look at together, including *I'm* (I am), *can't* (cannot), *don't* (do not), *You're* (you are), *that's* (that is). Find these together and point out how the apostrophes are used in place of the omitted letters.

Franklin Watts
First published in Great Britain in 2020
by The Watts Publishing Group

Series Editors: Jackie Hamley and Melanie Palmer
Series Advisors: Dr Sue Bodman and Glen Franklin
Series Designers: Peter Scoulding and Cathryn Gilbert

A CIP catalogue record for this book is
available from the British Library.

ISBN 978 1 4451 7175 3 (hbk)
ISBN 978 1 4451 7176 0 (pbk)
ISBN 978 1 4451 7311 5 (library ebook)

Printed in China

Franklin Watts
An imprint of
Hachette Children's Group
Part of The Watts Publishing Group
Carmelite House
50 Victoria Embankment
London EC4Y 0DZ

An Hachette UK Company
www.hachette.co.uk

www.reading-champion.co.uk

FSC
www.fsc.org
MIX
Paper from
responsible sources
FSC® C104740

Answer to Story order: 5, 3, 1, 2, 4